PELE'S
DOMAIN

This title is number five in the Frayed Edge Press Street Smart Series, published irregularly starting in 2019.

Other titles in the series include:

Full Fare by Jean-Bernard Pouy

Down and Out in Paris, with Cat by R.A. Bolo

The Accidental Anarchist by A.R. Melnik

Stealing MacGuffin by Matthew Kastel

PELE'S DOMAIN

Albert Tucher

Frayed Edge Press
Philadelphia, PA

Published by Frayed Edge Press in 2019

https://www.frayededgepress.com/

This book is printed on acid-free paper.

Interior illustrations by Bruce Orr

Publisher's Cataloging-in-Publication Data

Names: Tucher, Albert.
Title: Pele's domain / Albert Tucher.
Description: Philadelphia, PA : Frayed Edge Press, 2019. | Series: Street smart
    series ; 5 | Summary: The eruption of Kilauea on the Big Island of Hawaii tests
    Officer Jenny Freitas like nothing else in her young police career. After finding
    a murder victim in a doomed house just seconds before the lava overwhelms it, a
    second victim draws Jenny back to the danger zone again and again.
Identifiers: LCCN 2019955924 | ISBN 9781642510195 (pbk.) | ISBN
    9781642510201 (ebook)
Subjects: LCSH: Freitas, Jenny (Fictitious character) -- Fiction. | Murder --
    Investigation -- Fiction. | Police – Hawaii -- Fiction. | Policewomen -- Hawaii
    -- Fiction. | Hawaii -- Fiction. | BISAC: FICTION / Crime. | FICTION
    Mystery & Detective / Police Procedural. | FICTION / Mystery & Detective /
    Women Sleuths.
Classification: LCC PS3620.U34 P45 2019 | DDC 813 T83--dc23
LC record available at https://lccn.loc.gov/2019955924

Jenny's radio fussed at her. She unhooked it from her belt and kept moving through the house.

"Snap it up," said her partner. "It's getting bad out here."

"It's not so great in here, either. One more room to clear."

But the message got through. Cops didn't come any bigger or more stoic than Sammy Waga. When his voice took on that edge, they were running out of time.

She had never visited this house outside Pahoa before, but the layout of whitewashed Big Island boxes varied little. She tested the bedroom door with her palm. It felt no hotter than anything else in the superheated atmosphere. Neither did the handle. She turned it and pushed.

For a moment everything else yielded to the horror of what she saw. Jenny stared at the woman lying face up on the bed: her throat gaped open like another mouth, but this mouth was stretched in an eternal scream.

Jenny's cell phone seemed to have jumped into her hand. She started snapping pictures of everything in the room, finishing with a close-up of the woman's face with as little of the wound as she could get. This crime scene was doomed, and her phone would have to stand in for it. She couldn't help walking in the massive amount of blood, but she filed the thought away for the small hours of the morning.

"Jenny, now."

She backed out of the room and wiped her feet on the carpet before sprinting toward the front door. She couldn't afford to slip. Jenny yanked the door open and stumbled into hell.

1

The walls of the house had provided a little insulation against the worst of the heat. Outside, her face felt ready to melt. She looked toward Kilauea, which had been pumping lava on and off for years. But now Jenny couldn't trust the ground she stood on. Streets that children crisscrossed on their bikes had been splitting open without warning and hurling the boiling bowels of the planet into the air.

Just fifty yards away a glowing orange tide plowed through the rainforest. Some trees toppled, while others ignited where they stood. Splashes of lava leaped and sprawled like boiling surf, but no board in the world could ride this wave. The din assaulted her. Boulders banged together as the lava rolled them along. One rock exploded, and then another. Even as she ran, Jenny flinched and then wondered about the physics behind the phenomenon. If she lived through this, she might ask a geologist about it. Those were just the noises she could pick out of the crowd. They seemed to float on the roar of the earth's molten core.

She churned her feet faster toward the Hawaii County Ford Escape waiting in the clearing in front of the house. The passenger door stood open. Jenny dove into the front seat and landed with her head in Sammy's lap. Neither of them had time for embarrassment.

Sammy floored the accelerator and turned left hard. Jenny pulled her feet into the vehicle, as the passenger door's own momentum slammed it shut. She squirmed upright and looked back. The house was aflame, fully enveloped in a way that usually took minutes instead of seconds.

"Damn, girl," said Sammy. "What are you trying to do to me?"

"Do to you?"

"If the lava doesn't kill me, your mother will."

2

She churned her feet faster toward the Hawaii County Ford Escape waiting in the clearing in front of the house.

*****

"Run it down for me, Officer."

Detective Coutinho held Jenny's cell phone and thumbed through the pictures she had taken. His dark Portuguese face never gave much away. He could have been looking at snaps from her vacation.

She stood by his desk, swaying a little as her feet tried to get reacquainted with an old pair of shoes from the bottom of her locker. The crime scene techs had wanted the ones she had been wearing for the victim's blood and any other evidence they could find.

"Sammy and I were clearing the neighborhood."

Residents should have evacuated the day before, but there were always holdouts, as well as people so oblivious that the eruption would come as news to them, even as the heat built and volcanic gases clung to everything.

"So, we found this one guy at home. And he starts arguing with us—how come he has to go, and his neighbor doesn't? We went to check the other house out, but we didn't raise anybody. So, we figured we'd better go in."

Coutinho tapped the phone.

"Is she the neighbor?"

"The first guy was talking about a 'him.'"

It didn't prove much. The population of the Leilani Estates subdivision ebbed and flowed with cousins and friends of cousins who needed a place to stay for a while. Some houses were for rent by the month or week.

"Recognize her?"

He held the phone toward her, and Jenny looked at the image that already had an appointment with her nightmares. She hadn't managed to exclude the wound completely from the photo, which would have to be cropped if they needed to

4

show it to civilians. Jenny concentrated on the face, whose frozen horror must have turned to ash and disappeared under new volcanic rock by now. "Maybe. I have a feeling I might have seen her around."

But the woman's face was a quick course in Hawaiian history, combining Portuguese, Filipino, and Japanese genes. Jenny saw faces like it everywhere, including in her own mirror.

She swiped to the first photo she had taken, a framing shot of the woman on the bed.

"Look at this. Reminds me of a Viking funeral, the way she's laid out."

"Somebody put her there so she'd disappear."

"Sammy's a little pissed at me. We almost joined her."

Coutinho smiled.

"He'll come around."

*****

The next morning the first thing Jenny wanted to do was vomit. She didn't think it would help, and after a moment the urge retreated. The way her social life was going, it couldn't be morning sickness, but this must be what it felt like. She turned on the radio in her Camry in time to hear that her headache and nausea came from the gases that accompanied the eruption.

The announcer didn't have to sound so damned cheerful about it.

As long as the lava flowed, calling in sick wasn't an option. Another twelve-hour emergency shift beckoned. She forced herself to get out of the car and go into Ken's House of Pancakes in Hilo for breakfast as usual. Food was the last thing she wanted, but she couldn't afford to run out of energy halfway through the morning.

Conversation was sparse in Ken's. Most people were preparing for a routine day, but they were also trying to avoid thinking about the earth turning itself inside out just a half hour away.

At roll call the sergeant passed gas masks out. The eruption had slowed overnight, but it could pick up again in a moment.

By mid-morning she and Sammy had cleared recalcitrant residents from a dozen homes and delivered more than twenty people to the Pahoa Community Center. She was about to rejoin Sammy in their vehicle, when a man accosted her. He looked familiar, but his sheepish expression wasn't one he had been wearing the last time she saw him.

"Just wanted to say thanks, Officer. I acted pretty *lolo* yesterday."

"Mr. Tanaguchi, right?"

"Did you get my neighbor out?"

"Not exactly. Did you know him?"

"Just to say howzit."

"What made you think he was there in the house?"

"Saw him go in a few days ago. Hadn't seen him since. I just figured."

"Did you see anybody else coming or going?"

"Not lately. But I ain't the type to watch my neighbors twenty-four-seven."

People who felt a need to say that were exactly the type, thought Jenny. And they were eager to talk.

"That house was kind of a problem," he said. "Owner's never there. People rent it short-term, get up to stuff. You know da kine..." The all-purpose Pidgin phrase meant anything or nothing.

"The current tenant. What does he do?"

"Don't really know. He was less trouble than some of them."

"Jenny, we gotta go," Sammy called from their vehicle.

Jenny thanked the man for his time and then joined her partner.

"Where to?" she asked Sammy.

"Back to Leilani. Might not be as tense today."

They reached the grid of streets and turned toward the lava flow, which hunkered like a sullen crocodile the size of an Airbus. And that was just the small part they could see. A crust of brand-new rock had already formed on the beast, but dozens of glowing orange eyes gave glimpses into its pitiless soul.

For now, it was moving only inches per hour. She and Sammy started with the house closest to the flow. This time Jenny stayed with the vehicle. One of them had to. The lava could decide to speed up again without bothering to notify them.

She watched Sammy as he banged on the door and got no response. He went to the right side of the house and shaded his eyes with his cupped hands as he peered inside a window. He must have seen nothing out of line, because he went around back.

Seconds later he came back into view looking ready to heave, as if he had encountered a concentration of sulphur dioxide in the back yard.

"Another one," Sammy yelled to her. "Call it in."

"Another what?"

Sammy just shook his head, and a punch of adrenaline hit Jenny in the gut. She got on the radio.

*****

Coutinho stood looking down at the new victim.

"The lava was on our side this time. Wish I knew who to write the thank-you note to."

Jenny didn't remind him that the islands were the goddess Pele's domain, including their lethal innards. It might sound flippant.

This victim was giving her a worse feeling than even the very bad circumstances warranted. The woman also lay face up on the bed as if laid out for a funeral pyre, exactly like the first victim. Her throat was in the same condition. And both women were island ethnic mixes like Jenny herself.

This time the crime scene technicians were giving everything the complete work up, while Coutinho, Jenny, and Sammy searched the house. Jenny kept glancing out the window at the lava.

"Killed here," said Coutinho when they finished. "Like the first victim."

"Moke must have a vehicle," said Sammy. "Wouldn't want to get trapped here."

"Moke or tita," said Coutinho.

Bad guy or bad girl. Jenny had thought it herself but had decided not to bring it up yet.

"Can't canvas the neighborhood," said Coutinho. "Not after we made everybody leave. Question is, did the moke figure on that, or was he just lucky?"

"Or she," said Sammy.

Jenny decided she liked it when they did her job for her.

*****

But the next morning she was the one who found the first victim on a Facebook page set up for local residents to connect with each other and with loved ones. Jenny usually treated breakfast as personal time, but her habits had to yield to the emergency. And social media could hold crucial information.

"Has anyone seen my sister?" read the post.

Several photos of Rainie Fruehauf in happier times accompanied the query. Her sister Randi had posted from Las Vegas. Nothing surprised Jenny about that. At some point in history an economic refugee from Hawaii had landed a casino job in Vegas and then recommended his cousins and their friends, until the traffic back and forth had worn a trail in the ocean.

At headquarters Jenny found Coutinho alone in the tiny office he shared with Detective Kim, who had been detached to Kona Division for a while. Coutinho had been policing the eruption like every other cop, but his exhaustion wasn't showing yet.

"That's interesting," he said. "I tracked down the owner of the house and got the name of his most recent tenant. Gentleman named Malachi Pereira. He took off for Vegas right about the time when you were trying to save him from the lava."

Some detectives hoarded information, but Coutinho regarded a case as a teaching moment. With her, anyway.

"Sounds like he decided to leave in a big hurry."

"He left the place empty. And we know what they say about nature and a vacuum."

"Squatters," said Jenny. "I guess there's going to be even more of that for a while."

She thought about it.

"So did Malachi leave because of the murder, or did he just make an opportunity for somebody else?"

"We'll have to ask him when we find him," said Coutinho. He paused, as if preparing himself. "Right now, I'm going to reach out to the sister."

He typed into Messenger. "I doubt it will take long."

Jenny looked at her watch. She had five minutes before roll call. Maybe she could listen and learn. But four minutes passed before the phone on Coutinho's desk rang. He put it on speaker for her, which was also like him.

A male voice sounded from the phone. "Who's this?"

"Detective Coutinho, Hawaii County Police. Is Ms. Fruehauf there, please?"

"For why you want her?"

That single sentence identified the man as another transplant from Hawaii. Jenny thought back to what she had seen on Facebook and recalled an island face on a man hovering over Randi Fruehauf. He looked as if he did a lot of hovering.

"I really need to talk to her. What's your name, by the way?"

Suspicion traveled almost audibly across the ocean.

"Levi."

"Levi what?"

"Hold on."

"Hello?" asked a female voice.

"Ms. Fruehauf? I'm afraid I have bad news for you."

Jenny's watch told her she couldn't stay for more. Her disappointment was mixed with guilty relief. These notifications were part of the job, but she avoided them if she could. Coutinho would do the hard stuff and then fill her in about what he learned.

*****

The next morning at headquarters Jenny concentrated on putting her right foot forward and then her left. It amazed her how much this methodical approach accomplished against her exhaustion. Commitment and tenacity carried her into the station and halfway to the women's locker room, but Coutinho intercepted her.

"Need to pick your brain," he said. He studied her and added, "Over coffee."

She liked the sound of that. Drinking coffee would involve sitting.

He led her to the detectives' bullpen and pointed at an empty chair. For a giddy moment she felt like a little girl in Daddy's armchair, but that was a feeling she didn't intend to share.

Coutinho skipped the creamers and the sugar, and she did too, even if she would have preferred them. If drinking her coffee black was the price of admission to the big leagues, she would drink it black. She waited for him to start.

"Rainie Fruehauf was from Kona, originally. I remember you were detached to Kona Division for a while."

"Three months last summer," she said. "And you know what? That jogs my memory about our second victim. I saw her once coming out of a corporate crash pad in Keauhou."

Vacation condos packed the smaller town just south of Kona.

"J.D.L.R," she added. Just Doesn't Look Right. No cop needed it spelled out.

"No contact card?" asked Coutinho.

"I remember I was cuffing some moke. He didn't want to see things my way. I had to let her slide."

A contact card recorded an encounter that didn't lead to an arrest. If she hadn't been busy, Jenny would have stopped the woman as a way of telling her the cops knew a hooker when they saw one.

"She doesn't seem to have taken a bust. Her prints aren't in AFIS."

"How about Rainie Fruehauf? If I ever saw her, I don't remember."

"Her sister told me a lot. Rainie went through a bad patch. Lost a job, boyfriend ran out on her."

"Let me guess," said Jenny. "Taking the money and leaving the debts."

It was the story behind a lot of prostitutes at the escort level. In Hawaii they might earn three or four hundred dollars an hour, but little of it stuck to their fingers.

"What was the job she lost?"

"Housekeeper at a vacation condo complex in Keauhou. According to Randi, Rainie had an issue with a guest. A male guest who put the moves on her."

"It happens," said Jenny.

"But this incident happened at night, and she worked days. I didn't rub Randi's face in it, but it sounds like a hooker dispute with a john. The management of the place must have come to the same conclusion, because they didn't back her."

"Drugs?"

"The sister doesn't think so, but she didn't know about the other stuff either. According to her, Rainie was starting to get her act together. She mentioned a job offer on this side, which she liked because it wasn't in Kona."

"So, two hookers from Kona. Maybe ex-hookers. Both dead in Puna."

Jenny thought about the possibilities. The worst case was a serial killer, the kind who liked prostitutes because they made cooperative victims. Going off with strange men was part of the job description.

"What was she going to be doing?"

"Real estate."

"Heard that one, too." Hookers looking to transition chose a field that took anyone who was hungry.

"And," said Coutinho, "it can be as dangerous as hooking." More than one woman realtor had found herself alone in a property with the wrong man.

"I'm going to look at applications for realtor's licenses. See if Rainie was following through."

"And maybe there's another recent application. Somebody like our other victim."

Coutinho grinned. "Thought of that."

Jenny felt herself turning red. "I figured."

And of course, Sammy had to show up at that moment, when she was looking as if she had just asked Coutinho out on a date and been turned down.

"Can I borrow my partner, Detective?"

"She's all yours."

*****

For a second day the lava cooperated, and so did the local residents. The state had decided to let anyone who hadn't already evacuated stay for now, and in the shelters aloha prevailed. The cops held their breath about that, because nerves would start to fray sooner or later.

It didn't mean Jenny got a rest. It meant she went back on routine patrol. Women still went into labor, residents still called about ominous odors, and the mokes still looked for cars and homes to break into. So, she drove alone in her personal Camry with a blue cone on the roof and a backlog of mileage reimbursement forms under the seat. She found she missed Sammy's grumpiness and the way his three hundred pounds made the vehicle tilt toward him.

Dispatch sent her to a Toyota dealership with a complaint about a missing salesman and a RAV4 that might have gone with him. Jenny had bought her car at the same dealership three years earlier.

The sales manager remembered her. He should. He had been bugging her ever since to trade her car in, dangling some preposterous offer for a vehicle that already had more than fifty thousand hard miles on it.

"Officer, howzit?"

"Mr. Peres."

"You here about my missing vehicle?"

She had expected a little more tact from him about his priorities, but never mind.

"You also have a missing salesman?"

"Not a salesman. A *wahine*."

Jenny began to get that detective feeling.

"A woman."

"Yeah. I told them that on the phone."

"Things get garbled. What's her name?"

"Jackie Gutierres."

"What's she look like?"

"I can show you."

Peres led her to his office, where the usual group photos of the sales team decorated the walls. Jenny's eyes went straight to her second victim, third from the left. She couldn't help looking for a premonition of the victim's miserable fate, but it didn't show. It never did.

"When did you see her last?"

"Day the eruption started. Last time we had any customers to speak of. She took a prospect out for a test drive in my RAV. I hope she still has it."

"You're just reporting this now?"

"Been trying all week. Couldn't get through to anybody."

Unfortunately, that was plausible. "Who was the customer?"

"Kona guy. Little weird that he came all the way over here, but I'm not going to complain."

"You have the copy of his license?"

Peres opened a desk drawer and riffled files.

"Oswald Peltier. Keauhou address."

Jenny looked around and spotted two security cameras, one covering the entrance and the other the sales area. She would check outside for more surveillance.

"Those work?"

"Sure."

She got on the phone to Coutinho.

*****

Jenny stood behind the detective and watched the screen over his shoulder. Jackie Gutierres and the middle-aged man displayed an indefinable ease with each other.

"They've met," she said.

Coutinho paused the video.

"You're sure you never saw him before?" he asked Peres.

"Definitely. Remembering people is part of my job."

"What did he drive here? You must have tried to hold his car keys."

Peres grinned without shame, and Jenny remembered him trying that old car salesman's trick on her.

"He said a friend had dropped him off. What the hell, that could be good if he's marooned and desperate."

Coutinho grunted and restarted the video.

Jenny watched Jackie get up and leave the frame for a moment. The man waited at her desk. He was about fifty and impressively fit. Jenny had seen it before. The military had a major presence in Hawaii, and this man had put in his time, maybe in an elite unit. He looked around the showroom and for a moment gave the camera the perfect angle on his face.

"How smart is that?" said Coutinho. "He leaves his name and address and a mug shot."

"Well, he was thinking we'd never catch on. Both victims were supposed to burn up without a trace."

"True, but he's still way overconfident. Lucky for us."

Peres was looking more and more troubled.

"What's happened to her?" he asked.

"Mr. Peres," said Coutinho, "she won't be coming back."

He had the manager call up the exterior cameras. Jenny saw nothing but Jackie minutes closer to death, as she and the man drove away. He was a prudent driver, pausing to look both ways before pulling onto the highway.

Then the door opened, and a Japanese couple in their sixties came in. Peres got up and put on a salesman's smile that Jenny found grotesque in context. But his departure gave the cops some privacy.

"This raises some questions," said Coutinho. "Are there other victims we don't know about?"

"Let's make a list of jobs that are risky for women," said Jenny. "That could give us a rough idea."

She hadn't known she was going to blurt that out until the words emerged. But it was true. Sometimes a woman trying to make a living had to take a chance on a male stranger.

Prostitution wasn't the only such occupation. It just made the principle especially stark. And then there were the dangers posed by men who weren't strangers.

Coutinho raised an eyebrow and waited for more, but she had made her point.

"Well," he said, "we're letting people back into their neighborhoods to see what they can salvage. We'll just have to see what they find."

Pele must have heard that and found it funny, because she started the lava moving again that afternoon. Visits by residents were canceled, and the cops put their gas masks back on.

When Jenny climbed into the departmental Escape, Sammy gave her a dour look.

"Didn't we just do this?"

Underneath the words was grim anticipation of another body laid out on a bed. Every time Jenny pounded on a door or peered through a window, she held her breath. But she found nothing.

As they drove to the next street, Jenny's radio crackled, and Coutinho's voice said, "See if you can find Mr. Tanaguchi. Bring him in."

Jenny didn't ask what was up. She knew he wouldn't tell her over the radio.

"That's interesting," said Sammy.

Tanaguchi was still passing the days at the Pahoa Community Center. He seemed eager for a change of scenery, even at the police station. The desk sergeant directed them to Interview Two, where Coutinho met them.

"Can I get back out there?" Sammy asked.

That was Sammy. Detective stuff didn't interest him. Street policing did.

"Sure, Officer."

Coutinho had a civilian clerk set up Tanaguchi in Interview Two with coffee and a couple of malasadas from the best Portuguese donut truck in Hilo. He led Jenny to the hall outside the room.

"Randi Fruehauf is in the hospital. Somebody beat the hell out of her."

"She going to be okay?"

"It looked bad for a while, but they think so."

"How do we know about it?"

"When this first came up, I asked a Vegas detective if Randi had come to their attention. She hadn't at that point. But he remembered and called me back."

"Do they know who did it?"

"She says she didn't know him. Description could be anybody."

He called up a DMV photo on his laptop. "Here's Malachi Pereira."

"Did the Vegas cops find him?"

"We're behind the curve on this. He's back. United has him flying into Kona yesterday."

"Interesting," said Jenny. "Never seen him before."

"Let's see what Mr. Tanaguchi can remember."

The witness had just crumbs left from his donuts. "I never talked to Malachi that much," he said.

"He ever complain about business? Brag about it?"

"I don't think he was hurting for cash, but that's all I know about that." Tanaguchi paused for thought. "I know the guy owns the house. He complains about his tenants a lot, but Malachi didn't sound any worse than the rest of them."

"You see any visitors?"

"Yeah. Sketchy-looking mokes a couple times. Puna rats." Low-level local bad guys. "Matter of fact, one of them broke into my house a while back. Found him asleep on my couch. Whole place smelled like pakalolo."

"Did you get his name?"

"Nah. But I called you guys. It was funny as hell watching that big cop wake him up."

"Officer Waga?"

"Yeah. That's the one."

Jenny radioed Sammy, who remembered the incident.

"Harvey Koana. Wasn't even the first time I found him like that. When he ain't couch surfing, he's usually hanging at Isaac Hale. Should I bring him in?"

Coutinho nodded, and Jenny relayed the message.

When Sammy arrived with the young man, she recognized him. She spent a fair amount of time at the beach where small-time marijuana dealers spent a lot of theirs. In the interview room Koana struck a tough guy pose, which made Jenny feel even more tired. Coutinho seemed to feel the same.

"Harvey, spare us the attitude. Today we don't care about your business. We just need to pick your brain about Malachi Pereira."

The young man sat in sullen silence.

"Of course, we could decide to make a project of you. And if you make us go to the trouble, we're really going to come down on you. Clear?"

"Yeah," came after a moment.

"What's Malachi into?"

"What's anybody around here into? Pakalolo."

"Pimping?"

"How'd you know?"

"Harvey, we're the cops."

"He was bragging about that, but I didn't believe him."

"Why not?"

"Where's he gonna get these girls?"

"Seen him lately?"

"He just got back from Vegas."

"Why'd he go there?"

"No lava. What you think?"

"You stuck around."

"No cousins in Vegas."

"So, he's back."

"His cousin was getting on his nerves."

"Okay, Harvey, where's Malachi now?"

"I ain't his mother."

"Harvey. Remember what I said?"

"His house burned up."

"We know that."

"So, I don't know where he is right this minute. But I told him he could stay with me for a while."

"He take you up on it?"

"I'll know tonight."

"Harvey," said Coutinho, "when you see him, tell him we need to talk to him. And the longer it takes, the less he's going to like it when we find him."

*****

Police headquarters didn't look like home anymore.

The governor had finally activated the National Guard, partly to give the police a break. Many of the cops were starting to look like extras from *The Walking Dead*. But now military fatigues were showing up all over the station, as the Guard coordinated with the cops.

Coutinho had given Jenny coffee again.

"What's our next step, Officer?"

"I think we need to send a picture of Oswald Peltier to Kona. See if he's the man Rainie Fruehauf had the dispute with."

Coutinho smiled and nodded. "It'll be better if we go."

"We?"

"Yeah. Now that we have some help, we can act like detectives a little." He made a sweeping gesture that took in the military personnel and all the extra comings and goings.

Jenny had been looking forward to a day off, but an ambitious junior officer couldn't pass up an opportunity like this.

They left at five the next morning on little sleep, for Jenny, at least. The detective assignment had kept her mind working most of the night. Her body was clamoring for coffee, and when they reached the small town of Na'alehu near the southern tip of the island, she made herself look straight ahead. If she cast a longing look at the Punalu'u Bake Shop, Coutinho might think she wasn't ready for the big leagues. But he turned into the parking lot. "Malasadas are mandatory," he said.

The donuts didn't disappoint, and neither did the southern route to Kona, with the best ocean views on the island. In Kona they fought the local traffic to Division headquarters.

Coutinho led her through the gauntlet of male appraisal. These men hadn't seen her in the months since her detachment there had ended, and it seemed to make her new meat all over again. Jenny allowed herself a moment of relief at the prospect of going home soon.

Just ten minutes later a uniformed officer delivered the warrant they needed. The young man was even newer than Jenny's time in Kona Division.

"Thanks, Officer…" Coutinho looked at the young man's name tag. "…Bowman."

"Scott," said the officer to Jenny. He waited.

"Jenny," she said, wondering why it felt as if she had lost a point.

Coutinho drove, as they backtracked the few miles to Keauhou. Parking was always difficult there, with the condos occupying almost every square inch of ground. Coutinho somehow turned half a space into a whole one. Jenny climbed out of his Camry, and right away the sun began cooking her hair. By three in the afternoon she would feel ready for spontaneous combustion. These days she was getting enough of that feeling from the lava. Coutinho glanced at her and seemed to read her mind.

"At least the ground here cooperates."

Of course, volcanoes had created this side of the island too. They had been dormant for thousands of years, but Pele could decide to wake them up.

The manager of the complex was a Filipino bantamweight boxer type. Jenny played him some of the video from the Toyota dealership on her phone.

"That's Mr. Peltier," he said.

The manager took a key ring from a hook on the wall and led them across the interior courtyard to a staircase. On the second floor he opened a door for them. "All yours."

It wasn't going to take long. The place looked barely inhabited. Peltier didn't seem to have used the kitchen, even for pouring milk on cold cereal. The trash can was pristine.

"No TV," said Jenny. The bedroom held a single cot. "What was he, a monk?"

"Just military," said Coutinho.

That was a type they knew well.

Peltier did have a laptop computer, which rested on a card table in the middle of the living room. A folding chair and a desk lamp were the only other furnishings in the room.

Coutinho opened the computer, which started right up. Peltier hadn't password protected the screensaver or his files, and he had only one file in My Documents. Coutinho clicked on it and began to read.

"Interesting stuff," he said after a while.

He got up and let Jenny take the chair. The single file was hundreds of pages, and she decided to skim it first. But passage after passage grabbed her attention. She started reading some of them aloud.

"The people of Hawaii have lost their way, with their pollution and the destruction of their patrimony. Extinctions of the native species are a sign Pele will punish them."

"One of those," Coutinho said. He didn't have to explain. Many outsiders found island culture fascinating, but some became deranged on the topic.

When Peltier wasn't ranting, he reminisced about his transactions with local prostitutes. Jenny glanced at the cot in the bedroom and grimaced. It reminded her of college dorm sex on beds that could accommodate two bodies only if they were stacked.

Peltier's love of island purity and his attachment to commercial sex struck a dissonant chord, but he didn't seem to hear it. Three women came up repeatedly under obvious professional aliases. From his comments on their appearance, Jenny thought two were probably Rainie and Jackie, and the third a woman who resembled them. Jenny had known more than a few men who had a type when it came to women. If Peltier's type was one seen everywhere in these islands, that was convenient for him.

All three women had told him about their plans to relocate and get out of hooking. When Jenny had started meeting women in the business, usually while arresting them, she had been surprised by how much they talked to anyone who would listen, even johns. Maybe they did it to keep the silence of a strange man from filling the room.

Peltier seemed to approve of their plans. Jenny had seen that too. A john justified his hooker habit to himself by telling himself he was trying to help the women.

Then Pele dominated the ravings again.

"That would be the start of the eruption," said Jenny.

"The file was last updated a day into it," Coutinho replied.

"Harvey Koana said Malachi was pimping. Maybe he met Rainie and Jackie in Hilo."

"He could have been trying to draw them back into the business. Some of them relapse when they can't match the money they used to make."

Jenny thought about it. "

And when they did, Peltier got pissed enough to kill them?"

"This isn't hanging together yet. What we need to do is find the third woman, and hope she's in shape to tell us."

*****

The National Guard personnel were putting additional boots on the ground in the eruption zone, but they were also complicating things. Their culture differed from law enforcement. To get along with them, cops now had to become diplomats as well as doctors, nurses, lawyers, social workers, and maybe anthropologists and sociologists. And when it came to diplomacy, Jenny noticed a willingness on the part of male cops to defer to her.

Of course, it didn't stop them from doubting her abilities in other areas.

"The residents can leave if they want," she told a Guard captain at the Pahoa Community Center.

The captain was a woman from Honolulu, and she was making a point of acting like a hardcase. Jenny thought she might have something to prove to the men under her command, but that wasn't a police problem. Keeping the emergency shelters calm was, and running them like prison camps wasn't the way to do it.

"Then they head right back to the neighborhood," said the captain, "and we have to go rescue them again."

"Most of them won't. A few will, but, hey. If civilians didn't do dumb stuff, we'd be out of a job."

Jenny tried a man-to-man smile. It fell flat, but she thought she had defused the situation for now.

That was until she heard a female voice screaming outside the Center. Jenny hustled outside to see two young Guardsmen frog-marching a young woman toward the entrance. The woman was objecting in vulgar terms. Jenny planted herself in their path. The young men looked uncertain of their next step, and she thought she could get the initiative away from them.

"What's up?"

"Caught her in a house we already cleared."

"Doing what?"

The young man reddened, and his partner looked at his shoes. "She wouldn't say."

And they couldn't figure out how to make her.

"We thought you might know her," said his partner.

The Guardsmen looked disheveled, and Jenny saw scratches on their faces and forearms. The two young men had just learned the hard way that a small package could contain a lot of fight, and police work was harder than it looked.

"Okay, I'll take her."

She had never seen such relief on a young male face, not even when her father had been affable to her prom date.

Now Jenny evaluated her prize. She saw a basic island beauty with mixed ancestry, just like the two murdered women. And this young woman had been doing something in a no-go zone that she refused to talk about. Jenny could think of several explanations, but one had been on her mind a lot lately.

"What's your name?"

"Miriam."

"Miriam what?" Sometimes the game got exhausting, but a cop still had to play.

"Soares."

"How long have you been doing this?"

She made a point of using the vague phrase favored by women in the business. "How long have you been hooking?" would have sounded like a challenge and produced sullen silence.

The young woman still gave her a suspicious look.

"I don't care about your business," said Jenny. "Right now, I've got bigger things to worry about."

"Couple of years, off and on."

"Off and on?"

"I thought I was out of it. But waitressing wasn't paying the bills."

"Are you from Kona?"

"Yeah, how'd you know?"

"Do you know Rainie and Jackie?"

"Sure. Haven't seen them in a while."

Jenny reminded herself that a lot of people had been in no position to follow the news.

"You won't be seeing them," she said.

"Oh," said Miriam in a small voice, then something occurred to her. "I haven't seen Malachi, either. Is he okay?"

"Good question. Tell me about your client today."

"He found me on the message boards. Not through Malachi. Said he wanted something special."

"What was that?"

"Do it in the lava zone, with all the noise and stuff. He said it would get him off."

"And you said yes?"

"He said there was a thousand in it for me."

Miriam frowned.

"This is the second time we didn't connect. He's gonna find somebody else."

"When was the first?"

"Couple of days ago."

"You would never have seen the money. You're lucky those soldier boys found you first."

Miriam's mouth moved, but nothing came out.

"Know him?"

Miriam looked at the picture of Peltier.

"Yeah, that's Oswald, from Kona. A little weird, maybe, but nice enough. As they go."

"You seen him over on this side?"

"If you know everything, for why you ask me? Yeah, he found me at work. Said he was proud of me for making it. But then he wanted a date for old time's sake."

Miriam gave Jenny a look with sisterhood in it. "What is it with them?"

"Men?"

"I mean, it didn't surprise me, but why do they always try to have it both ways?"

"You figure that out, give me a call."

*****

"It's still not making sense," said Jenny. "She already knew Peltier. Why would he approach her online like a new john?"

"Digital trails are hard to get rid of. Maybe he knows that, and he wanted to look like somebody else—in case we ever caught onto it."

Coutinho didn't look as if he had convinced himself. Peltier had been careless with his name and face in the Toyota dealership. Now all of a sudden, he was a shrewd planner?

"Let's find him and ask," said Jenny.

"The problem is," said Coutinho, "it's a big island." Hawaii County cops said that a lot when a moke was eluding them.

"He didn't get his thrill this time," said Jenny. "Maybe we can get him to come to us."

Coutinho looked at her for a long moment. "You mean a decoy operation?"

"I'm his type. Like the other three."

"We need to think about this. I don't want your mother coming after me," he said, giving her a sharp look. "What?"

Jenny's smile widened. "Sammy's afraid of my mother too."

Coutinho didn't think about it for long. They had no alternative. "Let's set it up."

The internet had remade prostitution along with everything else. It took the tech people just an hour to give Jenny—or Leila, as she decided to call herself after the Leilani Estates—an online presence in *The Erotic Review, Best GFE,* and a website of her own. There were even templates available online for making escort sites.

GFE, she learned, stood for "Girlfriend Experience," a concept she would grapple with another time. The websites taught her another term: a "hobbyist" was a man who spent a lot of time and money on prostitutes at the escort level.

She and Coutinho settled in at a table in a coffee shop in the Prince Kuhio mall. They didn't know how tech savvy their suspect was, and they couldn't risk being traced to police headquarters. The detective was following the action on a clone of Jenny's laptop.

Leila already had messages. They expected a brief window of time before the hobbyist community realized she was virtual. By then they hoped to have made contact with the one john they wanted. The men were reckless with their personal information, which surprised Jenny but also helped in the screening process. A man who wanted her to come to his home or office or hotel room wasn't their target.

And then it arrived in an online chat room. "If you're feeling adventurous, you can make three times your rate. I'm talking about going to the lava zone. Up for it?"

Coutinho nodded to her. She decided not to remind him they weren't on the phone, and the moke couldn't hear them.

"Sure," she typed. "Where and when?"

He gave her an address in Leilani Estates.

"How about now?"

She and Coutinho had talked about this. She would need to stall the man to let her backup get into position without tipping him off.

"I have classes until two. Three o'clock?"

That was Jenny's idea. She had heard a lot of young women in this business posed as college students to give the johns some extra titillation.

"Okay, but no island time." He wanted three to mean three, and not whenever Jenny happened to get there.

"I didn't see any cops, but park a couple of houses away, just in case they come by."

"Three times my hourly rate is a thousand."

"It's a thousand, fifty," he typed back. "Don't sell yourself short."

"Smooth," Jenny said to Coutinho.

"It's not like he plans to pay you."

*****

Where had all these cops come from?

Jenny's friend Patsy Inaba used Coutinho's office to wire her up in privacy. When Jenny emerged dressed in her hooker outfit, every male officer in Hilo Division seemed to have nothing to do but loiter nearby.

She didn't get it. The modest top, shorts and sandals were nothing she wouldn't have worn off duty, which was the point. The street prostitutes of Waikiki were blatant about what they did, but women at the escort level dressed to blend in.

So, the men had come to peek at her looking like a whore who didn't look like a whore. And they didn't even seem disappointed.

Maybe sex is all in the mind.

"We don't really have anything on him yet," Coutinho said for the third time.

The repetition was a little annoying, but he was right. The Guardsmen had interrupted the suspect's plans for Miriam.

"Get him talking until he lets something slip."

"Got it."

"And if you even see a knife, that's it. You know what to say."

"Knife." She could probably remember that.

Her backup, officers borrowed from Kona Division, had already driven off in their undercover vehicles. No one was supposed to be out and about in the Leilani subdivision, but the local element that ignored the government on principle drove battered RAVs and Wranglers.

Sammy was too well known in Puna go undercover. He muttered some more about Jenny's mother and critiqued her appearance.

"Damn, girl, they should send me in. I look more like a hooker than you."

His flagrant concern touched her.

She was driving a Nissan Versa that Coutinho had found somewhere. Maybe Leila really was a college student. There was the house she wanted. Guard personnel had already scrawled "Clear" on it. She drove two houses past it and parked in the front yard.

Nobody in this normally nosy neighborhood came out to investigate. It was eerie.

As Jenny got out of the Versa and started toward the house, she read off the makes, models and license plates of six vehicles that didn't belong to her backup. Coutinho would run the plates. Residents had left some of them behind, but maybe one belonged to the man they wanted.

At the front door she paused for a moment to breathe and calm her butterflies.

"Going in," she said.

She pushed the door open, and right away the house spoke to her in a silent language that cops learned on the job. This wasn't going according to the plan. Jenny considered backing out, but she had only a feeling. If her instinct turned out wrong, and she aborted the operation for nothing, Coutinho's understanding would hit her harder than a reprimand.

She started going through the house room by room. Her hands felt strangely light and empty. She had spent the first twenty-four years of her life without a gun, but two years as a cop had wiped those years clean.

It had become habit to leave the bedroom and its nasty surprises for last. For that reason alone, she decided to shake things up and go there first. And of course, this time she found nothing.

That left the kitchen.

"Hi," said Jenny. "I'm Leila."

She knew the man at the table from photographs. Maybe that was why her voice stayed level, and her pulse didn't surge. In the flesh he still looked fit for his age, roughly fifty, and he perched on the chair like a man who didn't sit often, or for long. He would be hard to handle.

"I'm Oswald."

She hadn't expected him to use his real name. Maybe he wasn't concealing anything from her because he didn't intend to leave her alive. But somehow he didn't feel like a threat.

"We mentioned some money," she said.

He shook his head impatiently.

"I'm not him. I'm here to save your life. Not that my track record on that has been very good."

"Why do I need saving?"

Now was the time for his obsessive rant about saving her soul from the fate worse than death. But he shook his head.

"And I'm not one of those, either," he said. "I'm talking about your life, not your soul. He's already killed two friends of mine."

"Who?"

"Rainie and Jackie."

"No, who killed them?"

"That's the problem. I don't know."

His face let his frustration show.

"I just missed him the other day. He must have seen something that spooked him."

"Come with me," said Jenny. "We need to talk someplace else."

"You go. I'm going to wait a while longer. In case he still comes."

Jenny saw three choices. She could spend more time on persuading him, she could identify herself as a police officer, without knowing how he would react, or she could say, "Knife."

But Coutinho gave her a fourth choice, which was to do nothing. He appeared in the doorway of the kitchen with two uniforms behind him. One of them was Scott Bowman, the young man she had met in Kona. The other was probably a loaner from Kona as well.

Coutinho gave Peltier his stony cop look and then aimed it at Jenny. "You're both under arrest. Conspiracy to commit prostitution."

For now, he wanted to keep Peltier believing she was a hooker. She tried to look stoic and resigned, as if the occasional bust was part of her business model.

Bowman cuffed her. He did it right. Jenny hadn't felt steel on her wrists since her academy days, but the experience hadn't improved. The young men led her out of the kitchen and then out of the house.

The cuffs had to stay on until they were out of sight. Jenny found nothing to like about walking on tricky ground without her hands free to catch herself if she fell. But the young men kept a firm grip on her biceps. They walked her all the way to her Versa. Jenny rattled the cuffs on her wrists.

For now, he wanted to keep Peltier believing she was a hooker. She tried to look stoic and resigned, as if the occasional bust was part of her business model.

"Somebody want to get these off me?"

Nothing happened, unless young men staring and mentally undressing her counted as something.

"Um, today?"

Jenny kept her tone level and light. Showing concern would be a mistake.

But no one made a move toward her with the handcuff keys. A third young male officer appeared.

"The operation is over. So is the joke."

They kept running their eyes over her and in those eyes, she saw the reflected glow of the lava and something else as old as the planet: the glint of predators spotting their prey.

Would they really do something here? They were the cops, the people who were supposed to stand in the way of the pack mentality of young men. But these cops were also young men, and their adult supervision had already driven off.

She needed to suspend her disbelief. If this was a breakdown of civilization, she was a cop, and it was her job to handle it. She started planning her counterattack. It didn't look promising. She'd be lucky to get one groin kick in, and her flimsy sandals wouldn't accomplish much.

Which one would move first? Would guessing right do any good?

"Need some help, girlfriend?"

Patsy Inaba came bustling up to her with a key ready in her hand. In a moment Jenny's hands were free.

"You guys couldn't make yourselves useful?"

Jenny knew the tone of a woman making light of a situation that wasn't light at all. She had used it herself, hating herself as she did.

"Come on. Coutinho wants you."

Patsy hustled Jenny into her car. Neither spoke, until the young men began to shuffle away. Jenny started to breathe.

35

"Coutinho went back to headquarters," said Patsy finally. "He does want you."

"Okay." Jenny told herself to stop resenting Coutinho for leaving her. Not even he could foresee everything.

Patsy went to her vehicle. Jenny drove off and felt her heart rate slow. By the time she got back to headquarters, she had decided not to tell Coutinho anything about her close call, if that was what it was. He would believe her, but the young cops would support each other and simply say that she couldn't take a joke.

Patsy had done enough already; Jenny couldn't make her go public. But that left Jenny with one more thing to watch for over her shoulder.

She went to the bullpen. She didn't see Coutinho until she focused on the monitor for Interview Two. He was sitting across from Oswald Peltier.

"I read your diary," said the detective. "Interesting stuff."

"That's private."

"Not in a murder investigation."

"How many times I got to tell you? I didn't kill them."

"Several problems with that. You knew both victims. And now we find you right where we were waiting for the killer. How did you know where to be?"

"Educated guess. He's been using that neighborhood. I staked it out until I saw the young lady." Peltier looked proud of himself. "I know a prostitute when I see one."

Jenny's eyelids drooped with weariness. No one was around to hear Peltier's words, but he had immortalized them on video. Soon they would spread all over the station.

"Okay," said Coutinho, "if you didn't kill them, who did?"

"I'll tell you again. I don't know."

"Was it Malachi?"

"I never met him, but I guess it's possible. Maybe he found out they were working off the books. His books, anyway."

Peltier had a point. Pimps could turn murderous with a woman who cost them money.

Coutinho studied Peltier until the man started to squirm. "Let me show you something."

He opened a laptop on the table and turned it to face Peltier. Coutinho pressed play and sat back.

"That's you and Jackie Gutierres. Later that day she was dead. You want to explain what's going on here?"

"I was just looking in on her. She was at her new job, so I told them I was in the market for a car."

"Wasting her time like that?"

"I do need a new vehicle. I would have bought it from her."

"Who was the friend who dropped you at the dealer?"

Peltier didn't blink at Coutinho's detailed knowledge.

"I walked there, but car people think you're weird if you walk. Like maybe I don't know anything about cars, and they can overcharge me."

"So, you found Jackie and went off for a test drive."

"And we talked. She said she was doing well, but she offered me a date."

"Like old times."

"Right."

"So, where did that happen?"

"It didn't. She got a call on her cell. Then she said she had to do something. She'd make it up to me that night."

"What was it?"

"She didn't say."

"What do you think?"

"I think it was the killer offering her a lot of money."

"So, what happened?"

"She dropped me at my hotel and drove off."

"Anybody see this happen?"

"The desk clerk was looking right at us when I got out. She might remember."

Coutinho backed up and picked at Peltier's story, but he couldn't pry anything loose. He got up and said, "Sit tight, Oswald."

He came out and found Jenny in the bullpen. "What do you think, Officer?"

"I think I believe him."

"I do, too."

He could have looked happier about it.

"He was in the no-go zone. We can stretch the point and hold him for a while on that, but the…well, we don't want to think about it."

She knew what he meant. A cop shouldn't hope for another murder, but nothing else would move the case forward.

*****

Jenny had finished her shift and changed out of her uniform. She was driving home when her radio crackled and the dispatcher spoke. No one answered. Police manpower had stretched and finally snapped.

"I'll take it," said Jenny.

A cop was never off duty.

An anonymous caller had reported a man breaking into a house in the neighborhood. The caller shouldn't have been there to see it, but he had, and now someone needed to check it out. If it had been just a property crime, the cops could have practiced triage. But they were holding their breath about another murder.

Jenny stopped her Camry and looked toward the lava. It had taken another overnight breather, but it was now back to munching its way through forest, houses, cars and anything else it could find. Once again, she would have to move fast. She got out and approached the house.

The ground lurched sideways. Jenny flexed her knees and threw her arms out in a surfer's pose. But she was riding supposedly solid ground, not a wave. So this was what an earthquake felt like. The TV news reported minor temblors all the time, but this was the real thing.

She went through the steps—the knock on the door and then the circuit around the house, peering in through windows. Jenny then tried the front door handle, which turned. Someone had left in too much of a hurry to lock up—or maybe someone wanted company.

She radioed for backup, but she heard what she expected. "ASAP, Officer." The dispatcher didn't sound hopeful.

This was Jenny's show. She had to go in, but that didn't mean with her eyes closed. First, she cleared the other rooms, off-duty weapon in hand. She found nothing, but someone had just been here. She could feel it, even if she couldn't see it.

The ground shook again. This time she cringed at the noise of a jet liner revving its engines as it rolled up to the front door of the house. Okay, it couldn't be that, but it was the only comparison she could think of.

She went back to the front door and stopped just short of death itself.

A new fissure had opened up, and the blazing bowels of the earth were doing their best to climb out. Jenny grabbed the door frame to stop her forward momentum, as her eyes closed instinctively against the merciless heat. She forced them open to look for her car and a path to it.

Her Camry was gone. Pele had swallowed it whole.

"Bitch," said Jenny.

The goddess must have heard her. The lava leaped up from the fissure and reached for her with fiery claws.

As Jenny backed into the house, she looked to her left and saw the flowing lava closer than ever. For a demented moment she thought the flood from Kilauea intended to duel the fissure for supremacy. The winner's trophy would be Jenny, if she didn't get moving. She holstered her off-duty weapon for speed and ran through rooms as familiar as if she lived there herself.

The last thing she needed was an obstacle, especially one with the mass of this man. He was easily Sammy's size. Before she could stop, she ran right into him. He caught her bicep in a painful grip. Jenny leaned away and looked up at him.

There was a lot of him to take in, but she knew him. She had seen him on Facebook, hovering over Randi Fruehauf.

"Levi," she almost said, but she stopped herself. A better time to spring her knowledge on him might come later.

He stared down at her until she wondered whether he ever blinked. "Lava's getting close," she said.

"We have a few minutes."

"For what?"

"The cops saved you yesterday. I saw you getting busted. You and Peltier."

"He knows your name too. He must have told the cops. Don't make this worse."

"Save your breath. He doesn't know me."

"If you have the money, we can still do it."

"What money?"

He kept staring. Now Jenny understood the instinct that had made her keep up the hooker act. He would expect a cop to have a gun, but he might get careless with a prostitute.

His grip showed no mercy, but he was letting her angle her right side away from him so he couldn't feel her weapon against his body. Now she had to pick the right moment to use it.

Levi maneuvered her out of the doorway and started to drag her toward the bedroom. He looked away from her and toward their destination. The distraction gave her the opening she needed. Jenny drew the gun and fired into his side, under his right arm.

He roared with pain and shoved her away from him. Jenny fired again. Maybe she missed, or maybe the bullet gave up somewhere in his three hundred pounds of muscle and fat. He charged her, and she fired a third shot.

Then he was crushing her against the wall. Construction in some of these houses was so shoddy that for a moment she hoped he would propel her right through the sheet rock. But the wall held. He mashed her flat, until her breath left her.

Jenny's revolver had three rounds left, but they would do her no good if she couldn't free her arm to shoot. She tried to turn her body one way and then the other to win some room to maneuver. It wasn't working. Her arm stayed pinned down at her side.

But she found she could bend her right leg and slide it up the wall, which got her foot out of the way. She put a bullet into his left leg.

He bellowed again, but he kept pressing her into the wall. "Police! Don't move!"

The voice was young and male. Levi pulled her away from the wall, wrapped his arm around her, and tried to swing her in front of him. Jenny didn't plan to serve as anybody's human shield. She put another shot into his side, and when his grip loosened for an instant, she dropped and rolled.

And as she went, she got a look at her backup.

It was Scott Bowman. Scott, the would-be rapist.

He was aiming his S&W 9mm at Levi, who breathed hard and glared back at him.

"Down," said Scott.

The moment seemed to last hours, but then Levi got down on his knees. He walked forward on his hands until he was prone. He did it well for a man with five bullets in him. Jenny thought about the single round left in her revolver. It wouldn't have accomplished much without perfect placement and a lot of luck. Was she now going to need it for someone else?

Bowman took his handcuffs from his belt and tossed them to Jenny. She knee-walked to Levi and straddled his bulk as she cuffed him. Bowman kept his aim steady. Jenny nodded at him, and he took his radio from his belt. He called for more backup and an ambulance.

"Meet us outside Leilani."

The urgency in his tone got Jenny moving. She regained her feet and bent down to hook her hand under Levi's arm.

"Up. We have to go."

But he weighed three times her hundred and twenty pounds. She looked toward Bowman.

"Come on. Grab an arm."

He took Levi's other arm. They pulled in unison once, twice, three times, but the man was too heavy for both of them.

"Leave him," said Bowman. "We gotta get out of here."

"You're a cop," said Jenny.

Her tone lashed him into shamefaced fury. If Jenny lived through this, she had made an enemy for life. She looked down at Levi.

"Help with your legs," Jenny ordered him.

"I'm shot."

She knee-walked to Levi and straddled his bulk as she cuffed him.

"Whose fault is that?"

It took agonizing moments they couldn't afford, but Levi got his uninjured leg under him and supplied enough additional lift to get him upright.

"Out the back," said Bowman.

"No kidding," said Jenny. She didn't plan to challenge the fissure out front again.

"What kind of vehicle?" she asked.

"We've got an Escape."

Jenny exhaled in relief. The three of them would fit, assuming the limping six-legged beast they were making could get out of this house in time. She thanked Pele for the layout of a standard island box. She knew exactly where the back door was.

Halfway across the small back yard she heard a whoosh that penetrated the general din. She turned her head and saw the house fully aflame.

Bowman's departmental Ford Escape waited on the road behind the house. It took more sweating and cursing to heave Levi into the rear seat in his handcuffs, but she refused to trust him with his hands free.

Then she was in the passenger seat beside Bowman at the wheel, and the vehicle was moving. And within minutes she began to get that bad-date feeling. It stood to reason, with a man who had already proven he was someone to be avoided.

"I guess you're still on loan to Hilo," she said. Why was it always up to her to deescalate?

"Yeah."

Anger flared at his monosyllabic manly man bullshit. She put up with it every day, but maybe today was the day she had enough. Whatever it was, it was about to make her blurt.

She wondered what would come out, but she didn't feel like stopping it.

"We're cops," she said. "This is how cops act. We back each other up. You know it, and now I know you know it."

"You almost got us killed."

"Protect and serve. Even the bad guys."

He turned his head and glared, but she gave him her own cop look right back. What the hell. The best she could hope for was a stalemate, but maybe that was good enough.

*****

Coutinho found her in the waiting room at Hilo Medical Center.

"He's stabilized."

"Is he talking?"

"Not so far, but I don't think we need him to." He paused. "Randi Fruehauf admitted it: Levi was the one who beat her up. Wasn't the first time, but she had always stayed out of the hospital before. I checked the flight manifests, and he was here on our turf for both of the murders. She claims she didn't know."

"When he wasn't there to pound on her, she probably couldn't afford to wonder why."

"It would be nice if he felt the need to explain himself at some point. I mean, what was this about?"

"Maybe he came here so he wouldn't kill her. He wanted to keep her around for more punishment."

And here, with the deadly bowels of the earth to tell him murder didn't matter, Levi had felt at home.

"Nice guy," said Coutinho.

"I wish he was the only one."

About the Author

Albert Tucher is the author of the Errol Coutinho/Big Island of Hawaii series of novels, which includes *The Place of Refuge*, *The Hollow Vessel*, and *The Honorary Jersey Girl*. He also writes about prostitute Diana Andrews, who has appeared in almost 100 hard-boiled stories and the novella *The Same Mistake Twice*. He recently retired from forty years of public librarianship, and spends every possible moment in Hawaii.

Enjoyed this story? Read more from Frayed Edge Press...

Literature

Ambushing the Void short stories by James McAdams
*¿Cómo Hacer Preguntas? or How To Make Questions: 69 Instructional
    Poems (in English)* by Daniel Hales
Bellapalma by Jens Bjørneboe; translated by Esther Greenleaf Mürer
Ere the Cock Crows by Jens Bjørneboe; translated and with a
    reconstruction of the play by Esther Greenleaf Mürer
Rape Jokes by Louise MacGregor
Stealing: A Novel in Dreams by Shelly Brivic
The Splooge Factory poety by Christina Springer

History and Politics

*"Do Not Misunderstand Me": The Collected Radical Addresses to the
    Unity Congregation (1888-1891)* by Hugh Owen Pentecost
Jeremiah Hacker: Journalist, Anarchist, Abolitionist by Rebecca
    Pritchard
A Nurse's Story: Medical Missionary in Korea and Siberia, 1915-1920 by
    Delia Battles Lewis

Street Smart Series -- Short Fiction for People on the Go

Full Fare by Jean-Bernard Pouy
Down and Out in Paris, with Cat by R.A. Bolo
The Accidental Anarchist by A.R. Melnik
Stealing MacGuffin by Matthew Kastel
Pele's Domain by Albert Tucher

Visit us at: https://www.frayededgepress.com/